USBORNE WORLD WILDLIFE
MOUNTAIN WILDLIFE

Anna Claybourne and Antonia Cunningham

Edited by Kamini Khanduri

Designed by Andrew Dixon and Mary Cartwright
Illustrated by David Wright and Ian Jackson

Series editor: Felicity Brooks
Scientific consultants: Gill Standring and David Duthie
Map illustrations by Janos Marffy

D1592890

Contents

Mountains of the world

Mountains are some of the wildest places in the world. The tops of high mountains are often covered in snow, and the weather there is always cold and windy. Thick forests and steep, rocky slopes make it hard for people to live in mountain areas - but lots of different kinds of wildlife can survive there. Mountains are usually found in long lines, called ranges. The map below shows some of the world's mountain ranges.

Volcano erupting

Lava

Some mountains are volcanoes. When a volcano erupts, ash, steam and hot melted rock, called lava, burst out from under the surface of the Earth. The lava runs down the sides of the volcano.

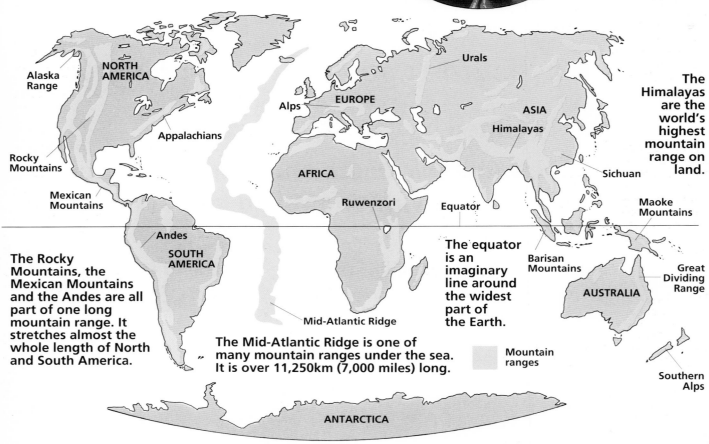

Alaska Range

NORTH AMERICA

Urals

Alps

EUROPE

ASIA

Himalayas

Appalachians

Rocky Mountains

AFRICA

Sichuan

The Himalayas are the world's highest mountain range on land.

Mexican Mountains

Ruwenzori

Equator

Maoke Mountains

Andes

SOUTH AMERICA

The equator is an imaginary line around the widest part of the Earth.

Barisan Mountains

Great Dividing Range

AUSTRALIA

The Rocky Mountains, the Mexican Mountains and the Andes are all part of one long mountain range. It stretches almost the whole length of North and South America.

Mid-Atlantic Ridge

The Mid-Atlantic Ridge is one of many mountain ranges under the sea. It is over 11,250km (7,000 miles) long.

Mountain ranges

Southern Alps

ANTARCTICA

Mountain sizes

These pictures show the different heights of some mountains around the world.

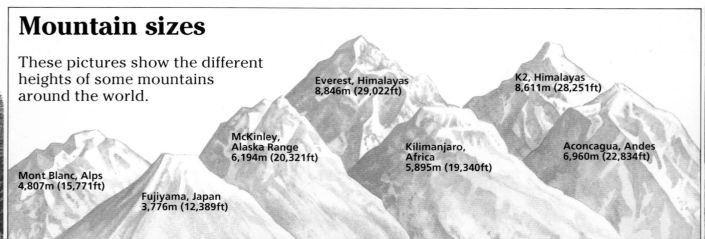

Everest, Himalayas
8,846m (29,022ft)

K2, Himalayas
8,611m (28,251ft)

McKinley,
Alaska Range
6,194m (20,321ft)

Kilimanjaro,
Africa
5,895m (19,340ft)

Aconcagua, Andes
6,960m (22,834ft)

Mont Blanc, Alps
4,807m (15,771ft)

Fujiyama, Japan
3,776m (12,389ft)

In the mountains

There are many kinds, or species, of plants and animals living in the mountains. The type of place where an animal or plant lives is called its habitat. Different mountain species live in different mountain habitats. Not many species live near the top of a high mountain because of the harsh weather. Lower down, where it is warmer and more sheltered, there is more wildlife. These pictures show the different levels on a mountain in North America, and some of the wildlife that lives there.

Some species of birds fly near the tops of mountains. They are mostly large birds that can fly in strong winds.

Golden eagle

Mountain goats and sheep live on the rocky slopes during summer. They can climb steep mountainsides and leap from rock to rock.

Rocky Mountain goat

Many bright flowers grow on the grassy slopes. Insects, such as bees and butterflies, fly among the flowers.

Apollo butterfly

Purple saxifrage

Mountain forests are home to many different kinds of wildlife, such as cougars, wolverines and porcupines.

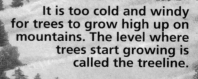

Cougar

The top of a mountain is called a peak. Many mountains have snow on their peaks all year long. The level where the snow ends is called the snowline.

Below the snowy mountain tops, there are often steep slopes covered with rocks and loose stones.

Below the rocky slopes, there are grassy meadows where small plants grow. Many animals live here.

It is too cold and windy for trees to grow high up on mountains. The level where trees start growing is called the treeline.

Beyond the trees

It can be hard for animals and plants to survive high up in the mountains. There are hardly any trees to give shelter, it is very windy and the ground is rocky and hard to cross. When the sun shines, it can get very hot, but at night the temperature drops below freezing point. Over millions of years, mountain animals and plants have gradually become well-suited to living in these harsh surroundings. This is called adaptation.

Ibex

Rock climbers

Ibexes spend most of the year in rocky areas high up in the mountains. They can climb incredibly steep slopes and jump from rock to rock, leaping over huge gaps. They eat tough grasses and other small plants that grow among the rocks. Sometimes it is hard to find enough to eat above the treeline, but ibexes can go without food for several days while they look for more.

Male ibexes show off their strength during the mating season by standing up on their back legs. They also fight over females, attacking each other with their long horns.

Ibexes have hooves with narrow edges that dig into cracks in the rocks, and slightly hollow soles that help them cling to rocky slopes. They have two toes which spread out when they land, making it easier for them to balance.

Goats and sheep

These goats and sheep are found in different countries but they all live in similar ways. They spend part of the year above the treeline. Their horns get bigger as the animals get older.

Mouflon

Markhor

Bighorn sheep

Tahr

Chamois

Rocky Mountain goat

Surviving the winter

Life is even harder for mountain animals in the winter. It is freezing cold, snow covers the ground and there is little food to be found. Many animals have very thick coats to keep them warm. Some also shelter inside a den or burrow.

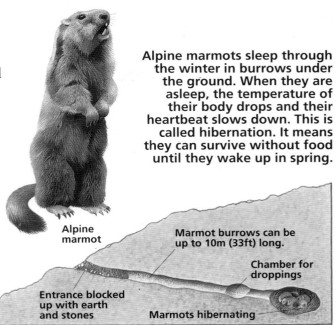

Alpine marmots sleep through the winter in burrows under the ground. When they are asleep, the temperature of their body drops and their heartbeat slows down. This is called hibernation. It means they can survive without food until they wake up in spring.

Alpine marmot

Snow leopards live high up in the mountains of Asia. They have thick fur all over their bodies, even on the soles of their feet. Snow leopards shelter in dens between rocks, but often come out to find food.

Marmot burrows can be up to 10m (33ft) long.

Chamber for droppings

Entrance blocked up with earth and stones

Marmots hibernating

Making hay

Pikas are small animals that live on rocky slopes high up in the mountains of North America and Asia. In the winter, they feed on dried plants, or hay, that they have stored up the summer before.

During the summer, a pika collects grass and other plants to store for the winter. It is easier to find food in warm weather.

The pika carries bundles of plants to a rock and lays them out to dry. Dried plants, or hay, keep longer than fresh ones.

The pika guards its food while it dries, because other pikas may try to steal it. It sniffs the air, and lifts its head to look around.

Moving away

In the winter, red deer move down the mountain to live in the forests until spring. The male deer, called stags, go down first. Large groups of females, called hinds, follow a few weeks later. They travel in long lines of up to 500 animals.

Male deer have large horns, called antlers. These drop off every spring. It takes about three months for a new pair to grow.

Red deer stag

Red deer hinds moving down the mountain

Yaks

Yaks are huge, hairy relatives of cows. They live high up in the mountains of Asia and eat grass and other plants. Their thick coats help protect them from the freezing cold, but they also have another good way of keeping warm. Their stomachs give out heat when they digest, or break down, food. This warms the yaks' bodies from the inside.

Yaks have long, shaggy coats that almost touch the ground. Their horns start growing when they are about two years old.

Female yak

In Nepal and Tibet, people keep yaks as farm animals. They use them for carrying heavy loads up and down mountainsides. They also get milk and butter from them.

Baby yaks are called calves. Yaks usually have only one calf at a time.

Yak calf

Mosses and lichens

On high mountain slopes, the soil is thin and stony. Above the grassy meadows, there are not many plants. Only mosses and lichens can survive very high up. They usually grow on rocks close to the ground, where it is less windy.

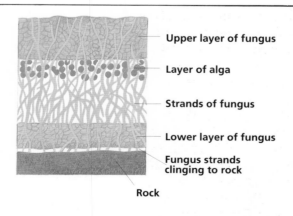

Upper layer of fungus

Layer of alga

Strands of fungus

Lower layer of fungus

Fungus strands clinging to rock

Rock

Mosses

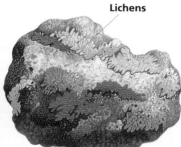

Lichens

The picture above shows how lichens are made up of an alga and a fungus living together. The fungus surrounds the alga and helps it to stay moist. The alga makes food for itself and for the fungus.

Tails for jumping

Springtails are tiny insects. They live in shallow soil and feed on dead plants. They can survive cold weather because they have a chemical in their bodies which stops them from freezing. They use their strong tails to jump short distances.

Tail

When a springtail is crawling around or standing still, its tail is folded under its body.

When it wants to jump, it flicks its tail down onto the ground very quickly and suddenly.

By pushing its tail against the ground, the springtail jumps up into the air.

Small mammals

These pictures show three small mammals that live above the treeline. Mammals are animals that give birth to live young instead of laying eggs. Baby mammals feed on their mother's milk. All mammals need to keep warm, but small mammals lose heat from their bodies more quickly than larger ones. They need very thick fur to keep out the cold.

Chinchilla

Chinchillas live in South America. They have very thick, soft fur, with up to 60 hairs growing out of each tiny hole, or pore, in their skin. Most mammals have only one hair in each pore.

Mountain viscacha

Mountain viscachas live in South America. They sleep in cracks between rocks. During the day, they often sit in the sunshine to keep warm.

Hoary marmot

Hoary marmots live in North America. They dig underground burrows, where they sleep at night. They also use their burrows as hiding places if they are in danger.

Birds of prey

Birds of prey, such as falcons, eagles and hawks, feed on other birds or on small mammals. Many species live above the treeline. They often build nests on rocks, or in shallow holes in the ground. Sometimes they use another bird's old nest. Birds of prey have very good eyesight. Most hunt during the day, so they can see their prey from far away.

Gyrfalcon feeding on a pigeon

Gyrfalcons fly near the ground to chase their prey. Then they grab it with their large claws and tear it apart with their strong beaks.

7

Forests in the north

In the most northern parts of the world, the summers are very short and the winters are very long and freezing cold. Only trees such as firs, spruces and pines can grow on the mountains there. These types of trees are called conifers. Many animals move down to the conifer forests in the autumn, because the trees provide food and shelter during the winter. This picture shows part of a conifer forest high in the Rocky Mountains in North America.

Goshawks hunt small animals, including other birds.

Goshawk

Bluebird

Conifers

Conifers are well adapted to cold weather. Their needles are tougher than ordinary flat leaves, so they can keep growing in winter. Conifer seeds are hidden inside a hard cone.

Cone cut in half

Hard scales

Seed

Conifer trees are shaped so that snow can slide off their branches.

Every winter, snowshoe hares grow an extra-thick coat of white fur to keep them warm.

Snowshoe hare

Red crossbills use the crossed tips of their beaks to break into cones and reach the seeds inside.

Red crossbill

Wapiti

Wapiti are a kind of deer. They eat small plants, tree bark and leaves. Every year, each male's antlers fall off and another pair grows.

Spruce grouse eat pine needles.

Woodpeckers peck holes in tree trunks to find insects.

Hairy woodpecker

Wolverine

Wolverines eat other animals, such as hares and young deer.

Mushrooms, mosses and lichens grow on the dry, cold ground under the snow.

Chanterelle mushrooms

In winter, porcupines eat pine needles and tree bark. They shelter between tree roots or in hollow logs.

North American porcupine

Animal tracks can be seen in the snow.

Wolverine tracks

The mating season

Wapiti spend the summer above the treeline, and the winter in conifer forests. Male and female wapiti usually live in separate groups. They mate every year in September. Their mating season is called the rut.

At the start of the rut, a stag (male wapiti) gets restless. He leaves his group and goes off on his own.

The stag goes to look for some hinds (females). He roars very loudly to let other stags know he is there and to show off his strength.

The stag thrashes his antlers against the trees. He rounds up a large group of hinds to mate with.

He fights other stags that try to take his hinds, locking his antlers with theirs in a test of strength. The winner stays with the hinds.

Mountain rainforests

Near the equator, the weather is usually hot and damp. Thick, wet forests, called rainforests, grow there. They are home to thousands of different kinds of animals and plants. Rainforests that grow on mountain slopes often have their own wildlife species. The map below shows the mountain rainforest areas of the world.

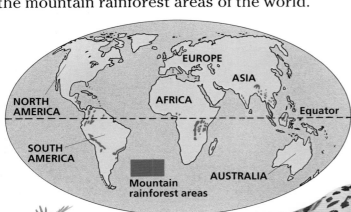

Mountain anoa

Mountain anoas only live on one island, called Sulawesi, in Southeast Asia. They are so rare that scientists have found out very little about them.

Leopards live in many different habitats in Africa and Asia, including mountain rainforests. They eat animals such as lizards, birds, deer and monkeys. They are good at climbing and sometimes drag their prey up into trees to eat it.

Leopards feeding

Chameleons

Jackson's chameleons live in African mountain rainforests. They creep slowly along branches to hunt for insects.

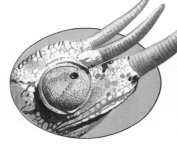

A chameleon can keep its body still and swivel its huge eyes around in different directions, to look for prey.

If it sees an insect, such as a fly, the chameleon suddenly shoots out its long, sticky tongue to catch it.

The fly sticks to the end of the chameleon's tongue. Then the chameleon pulls its tongue back into its mouth and eats the fly.

Apes and monkeys

There are many different kinds of apes and monkeys living in the mountain rainforests of Asia, Africa and South America. Apes, such as gorillas and chimpanzees, have no tails. Monkeys have tails, and are usually smaller than apes. Several monkey species have very strong tails which they use like an extra arm, for holding onto branches. These are called prehensile tails.

De Brazza's guenon

Hanuman langur

Woolly monkey

Black and white colobus monkey

Stump-tailed macaque

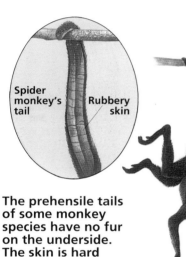

Spider monkey's tail

Rubbery skin

Prehensile tail

Spider monkey

Owl-faced monkey

The prehensile tails of some monkey species have no fur on the underside. The skin is hard and rubbery, with ridges. This helps the monkey to grip onto branches.

Chimpanzees

Francois's langur

Mountain gorilla

Mountains of the Moon

The Ruwenzori mountains in Africa are sometimes called the Mountains of the Moon. Rainforests grow on their lower slopes but higher up, there are strange forests of giant flowers. Some species of groundsel and lobelia grow up to 9m (30ft) high in the Ruwenzori. In most other places, these types of plants only grow to about 0.6m (2ft) high.

Giant lobelia

Giant groundsel

Giant earthworms live in the soil near rivers in the Ruwenzori mountains. They can grow to 75cm (2.5ft) long.

Water wildlife

When rain falls on the mountains, it runs into small, fast-flowing streams. These rush down the mountainsides and join together to become rivers. Cold, clear mountain lakes form in the valleys between the slopes. Many different wildlife species live in and around streams, rivers and lakes. The picture on these pages shows a mountain stream in Europe, and some of the wildlife that lives there.

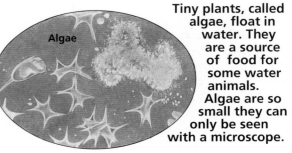

Tiny plants, called algae, float in water. They are a source of food for some water animals. Algae are so small they can only be seen with a microscope.

Algae

Insects

Many insects live near mountain streams. Some of them lay their eggs in the water. When the young insects hatch, they live in the water until they are almost fully grown. Then they climb out and turn into adults by shedding their skins.

Young insects are called larvae or nymphs. They often look very different from the adults.

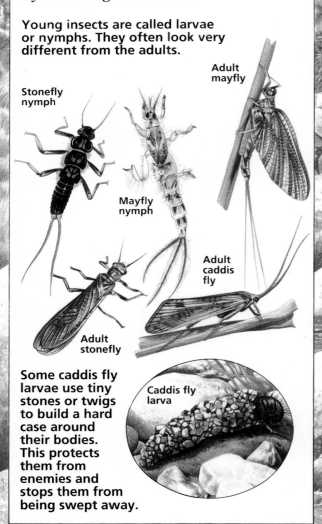

Stonefly nymph

Adult mayfly

Mayfly nymph

Adult caddis fly

Adult stonefly

Some caddis fly larvae use tiny stones or twigs to build a hard case around their bodies. This protects them from enemies and stops them from being swept away.

Caddis fly larva

Waterfall

There are often lots of plants near waterfalls. The splashing water makes the ground damp, so it is easy for them to grow there.

Dippers often stand on stones in streams.

Dipper

Otters

Otters live in burrows, called holts, near streams and rivers. They often swim underwater to catch fish.

Dippers

Dippers feed on insects and snails that live on the stream bed. They run down the side of a rock into the water, or dive in head first, with their eyes open.

Once they are underwater, dippers spread their wings to keep their balance in the fast-flowing stream. They walk along the bottom, looking for food among the stones.

If a dipper finds an insect or a snail, it catches it in its beak. It quickly hops out of the water and stands on a rock to eat its food. Then it goes underwater again.

Many animals come to mountain streams to drink.

Red deer

Water moss grows on rocks. It can live above and below the water surface.

Water moss

Underwater life

In mountain streams, the water flows very quickly. Large fish are strong enough to swim against the flow, but small ones have to cling to rocks or hide under stones to avoid being swept away. Fish also live in mountain lakes, where the water does not move very fast.

Bullheads lie on the stony stream bed. The water flows more slowly there, so they do not get swept away. Their spotted skin helps them blend in with their surroundings.

Bullhead on the stream bed

Stone loaches

Stone loaches cling to rocks with their mouths to stop themselves from being swept away.

Crayfish live under stones in streams and rivers. In spite of their name, they are not fish, but are related to crabs and lobsters.

Crayfish

Charr

Charr live in high mountain lakes. The males have very bright markings.

Amazing journeys

Salmon lay their eggs in mountain streams. The newly hatched salmon stay in the stream for up to six years, then swim down to the sea. A few years later, they return to their home stream to lay their eggs. The pictures below show Atlantic salmon.

The salmon leave the sea and swim up the river that leads to their home stream. Scientists think they may find their way partly by the smell and taste of the water.

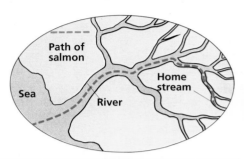

The salmon have to be very strong to survive the long journey upstream. They do not eat anything on the way. Some of them become exhausted and die on the journey.

During the journey, the salmon leap over waterfalls and rocks. They can jump as high as 3m (10ft) in the air, using their tails to push themselves out of the water.

When the salmon arrive at their home streams, each female flaps her tail on the stream bed to make a hollow, called a redd. She lays up to 15,000 eggs in it.

When the baby salmon, called fry, hatch out, they feed on the yolks of their eggs, which are still attached to them. Later, the yolks drop off and the fry feed on insects.

Fishing for salmon

In Alaska in North America, brown bears fish for Pacific salmon which swim up mountain rivers to breed. For most of the year, bears eat leaves, berries, honey and insects and other animals. When they get the chance to eat salmon, they eat as much as possible. The bears catch fish in several different ways.

Bears learn to fish when they are very young.

Some bears snap up the fish in their jaws.

Some bears use their paws to flip the fish out of the water and into their mouths.

Some bears dive into the water, pin the fish to the river bed with their paws, and then grab them with their teeth.

Flamingos in the Andes

High in the Andes mountains in South America, there are large, shallow lakes which are home to big groups of flamingos. The flamingos feed on tiny plants and animals that live in the water and in the mud at the bottom of the lakes.

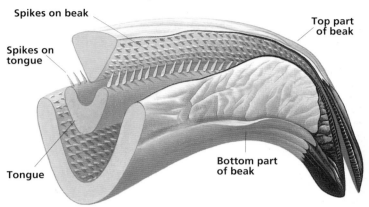

Spikes on beak

Spikes on tongue

Top part of beak

Tongue

Bottom part of beak

The picture above shows part of a flamingo's beak. When a flamingo feeds, food sticks to small spikes on the inside of its beak. The flamingo quickly scrapes the food off, using larger spikes on its tongue. Then it swallows the food and pushes the water and mud back out of its beak.

Flamingos feed with their heads upside-down. They stick their beaks into the mud, and suck in a mixture of water, mud and food.

Mountain monkeys

Japanese macaques are a species of monkey. They are sometimes called snow monkeys. They live in Japan in mountain forests and on rocky slopes. Macaques spend a lot of time playing and swimming in rivers and streams. In some parts of Japan, there are places called hot springs, where warm water comes out of the ground. The macaques sit in the hot water during the winter, to keep warm.

Sometimes, macaques spend nearly all day sitting in the hot springs. When it is very cold, snow may fall and settle on their heads. Macaques often sit in the hot water right up to their necks.

Acid lakes

The water in mountain lakes is not always clean. If there is pollution in the air, this may fall into lakes as acid rain or snow (see page 31). Fish cannot live in polluted water. Other animals may also die if there are not enough fish for them to eat.

Acid lakes often look clean, but very little wildlife can survive there.

Hunting and escaping

In every habitat, there are predators - animals that hunt other animals for food. The animals that they hunt are called prey. In mountain areas there are lots of species of predators, such as bears, wolves, birds of prey and big cats. Different predators hunt in different ways and prey animals have lots of different ways of trying to escape. One way of showing which animals eat what is by a food web. The picture below shows part of a food web in a North American mountain habitat. (The pictures are not to scale.)

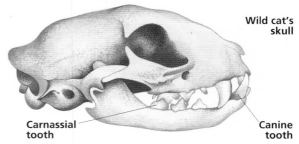
Wild cat's skull

Carnassial tooth

Canine tooth

Like many predators, wild cats have teeth that are well-suited to eating meat. They have long canine teeth for biting and killing, and sharp carnassial teeth for slicing and chewing.

The arrows point from the plant or animal that is eaten to the animal that eats it. For example, mayfly nymphs are eaten by salmon, and salmon are eaten by brown bears.

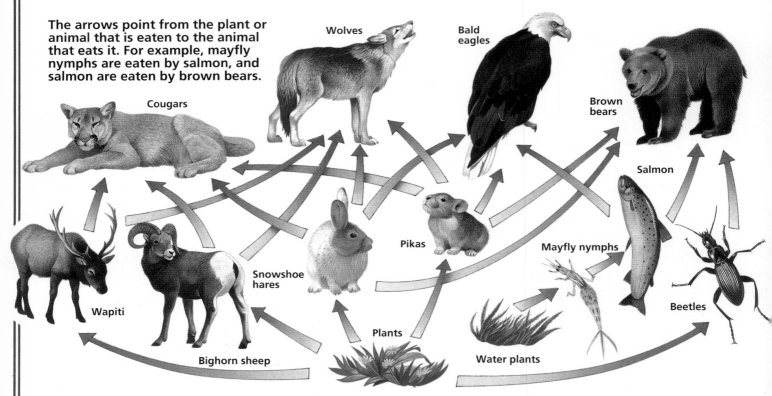

Wolves

Bald eagles

Brown bears

Cougars

Salmon

Pikas

Mayfly nymphs

Snowshoe hares

Beetles

Wapiti

Plants

Bighorn sheep

Water plants

Hunting in groups

Wolves live in mountain forests in many parts of Asia and North America. They live in groups, called packs. A wolf cannot kill big animals on its own, so the wolves in a pack often go hunting together.

These wolves have smelled a deer somewhere nearby. They can tell exactly where the deer is by picking up its scent.

The wolves approach the deer in a long line, with the wind blowing in their direction so the deer cannot smell them.

When the deer sees the wolves, it starts running. The wolves chase after it and surround it, cutting off its escape route.

If the wolves catch the deer, they attack it, drag it to the ground and kill it. Then they eat it as quickly as possible.

Territories

Many predators mark out an area of land for themselves, by leaving droppings and scratching on trees with their claws. This area is called a territory. Each animal hunts in its own territory, so there are not too many predators of the same species competing for the same prey. Males do not usually go into each other's territories.

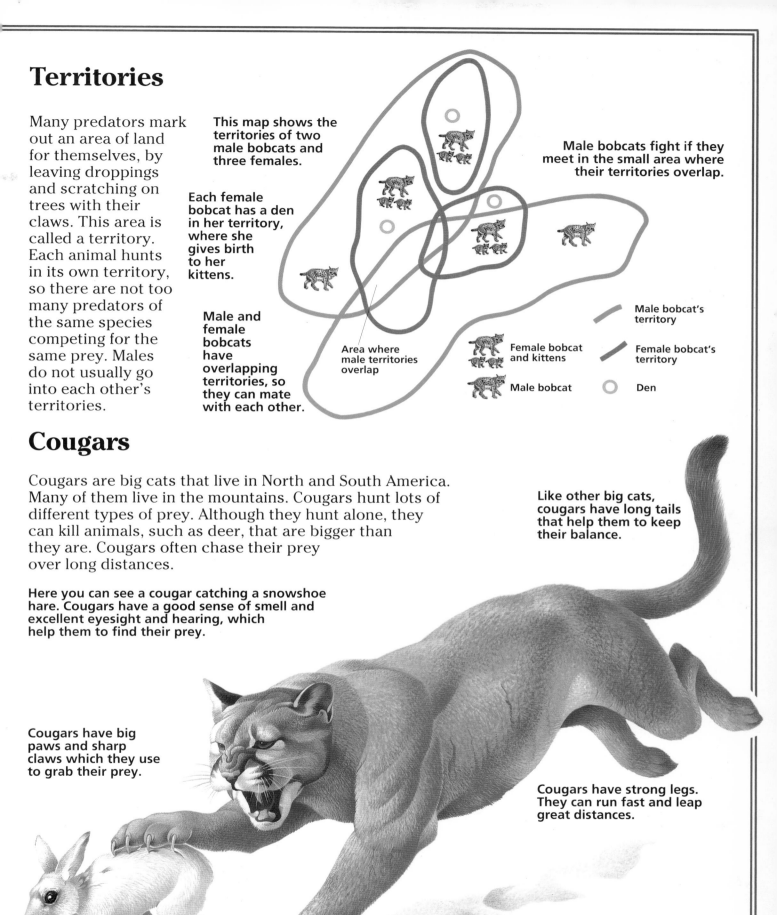

This map shows the territories of two male bobcats and three females.

Each female bobcat has a den in her territory, where she gives birth to her kittens.

Male and female bobcats have overlapping territories, so they can mate with each other.

Area where male territories overlap

Male bobcats fight if they meet in the small area where their territories overlap.

Female bobcat and kittens

Male bobcat

Male bobcat's territory

Female bobcat's territory

Den

Cougars

Cougars are big cats that live in North and South America. Many of them live in the mountains. Cougars hunt lots of different types of prey. Although they hunt alone, they can kill animals, such as deer, that are bigger than they are. Cougars often chase their prey over long distances.

Here you can see a cougar catching a snowshoe hare. Cougars have a good sense of smell and excellent eyesight and hearing, which help them to find their prey.

Like other big cats, cougars have long tails that help them to keep their balance.

Cougars have big paws and sharp claws which they use to grab their prey.

Cougars have strong legs. They can run fast and leap great distances.

Avoiding predators

Animals that are hunted by other animals do not always get caught. They escape by running away, hiding or fighting back at their enemies. Some animals, though, have more unusual ways of avoiding being eaten.

Snowshoe hares are hunted by many kinds of predators. They are specially adapted to spotting predators and running away fast.

Big ears to listen for predators

Good eyesight to spot approaching predators

Strong back legs help hares to run and jump fast.

Snowshoe hares have big, flat back feet which help to stop them from sinking in soft snow.

Hairs on soles of feet give extra grip on slippery ground.

These pictures show how a hare leaps along.

It lands on its front feet.

Then it puts its back feet down in front, and leaps again.

The hare leaps forward, taking off from its back feet.

Camouflage

Many animals match their surroundings, so predators cannot see them so easily. This is called camouflage. Some mountain animals also change their appearance with the seasons, so they can blend with different backgrounds at different times of the year.

Common green grasshoppers are well-camouflaged on the grassy meadows where they live.

Ptarmigan in summer

Ptarmigans grow white feathers in winter, to blend with the snow, and speckled brown feathers in summer, to blend with the rocks and plants.

Ptarmigan in winter

Porcupines

If porcupines are attacked, they defend themselves in an unusual way. They are covered with sharp spines, or quills, which come away from the porcupine's skin if they are touched.

When there is no danger, a porcupine's quills lie flat against its body, pointing in the same direction as its tail.

When the porcupine sees a predator, such as a cougar, its quills stand on end, or bristle, and point in all directions. This frightens most predators away.

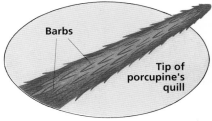

Barbs

Tip of porcupine's quill

If a predator does attack, some of the porcupine's quills may stick into it. Each quill has tiny spikes, called barbs, on its tip. These dig into the predator's skin and make it very painful to pull the quill out again.

Playing tricks

Some animals use tricks to avoid being eaten. Some species pretend to be dead if they see a predator. Most predators only eat prey they have killed themselves, so they leave the animal alone. Other species have markings that make them look like more dangerous animals. This often frightens predators away.

Ringed snakes live on boggy hillsides in Europe. When a predator is nearby, they pretend to be dead. They lie coiled up with their heads upside-down and their tongues hanging out.

Emperor moths have two spots on their wings that look like a large pair of eyes. Birds that eat moths are frightened away, because the moth looks like the face of a much bigger animal.

Safety in numbers

Animals are often safer from predators if they live in groups. The members of a group can warn each other if there is danger. In some species, one animal gives a warning call if it sees a predator approaching. This gives the rest of the group a chance to hide.

In the African mountains, groups of rock hyraxes often lie together in the sun. If one hyrax sees a predator, such as a snake or an eagle, it makes a loud screaming call to warn all the others.

Hyrax making a warning call

Mountain birds

Hundreds of species of birds live in mountain areas. Big birds of prey, such as eagles, often live high up on rocky slopes. They can fly in strong winds without being blown away. Smaller birds usually live in the meadows and forests lower down. In the winter, many mountain birds move away to warmer areas. Some fly incredibly long distances, often to other countries. These journeys are called migrations. These pictures show some birds that spend the summer in mountains in different parts of Europe.

Grey wagtail

Alpine swift

Dotterel

Wood warbler

Crag martin

Red-throated pipit

Snow bunting

Alpine accentor

House martin

Siskin

Redpoll

Greenshank

Rock thrush

Wheatear

Bluethroat

Ring ouzel

Staying all winter

Some birds stay in the mountains all year long. Wallcreepers spend the summer high up among the rocks and snow, and move a little lower down the mountain for the winter. Snow finches usually stay high up all winter, and only move down the mountain if the weather is extremely cold.

Wallcreepers grip the sides of cliffs with their large claws, and use their long beaks to search for insects in cracks between the rocks.

Wallcreeper

Snow finches feeding

Snow finch fluffing out its feathers

Snow finches feed in large flocks. In winter, they often go into mountain towns and villages, where people may feed them. They fluff out their feathers to keep warm.

Showing off

Horns

Lappet

The males of some bird species dance and show off their bright markings to attract females. These performances are called courtship displays. Temminck's tragopans, which live in Chinese mountain forests, perform amazing displays.

When a male Temminck's tragopan displays, he opens out his chest feathers and shows a bright blue and red flap of skin, which is called a lappet. Two soft horns stand up on the top of his head.

The male tragopan's lappet is hidden under his red feathers when he is not displaying.

Group displays

Black grouse live in forests and meadows on mountains in Europe. The males perform noisy courtship displays in a group. The area where they display is called a lek. Female black grouse, called greyhens, come to the lek to watch the males.

This picture shows a black grouse lek. The males call loudly and display in several different positions. The positions have different names.

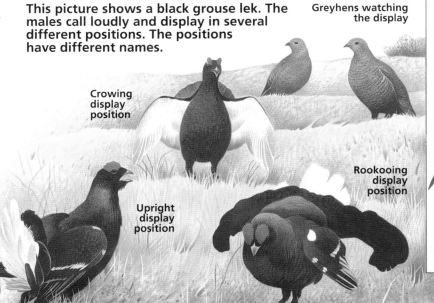

Greyhens watching the display

Crowing display position

Upright display position

Rookooing display position

Building a nest

Birds need somewhere safe to lay their eggs. In forests, most birds build nests in trees. Above the treeline, it is harder to find good nesting places. Like other animals, mountain birds have become adapted to their surroundings. They nest in different ways, depending on their habitat.

Anna's hummingbirds live in mountain forests. The female uses lichens and plants to build a tiny nest in a tree. She ties the nest onto a branch with spider's webs, to stop it from being blown away.

Ptarmigans live mainly above the treeline. They make their nests on the ground, in a hollow lined with grass and feathers. The nest is often hidden among rocks or bushes, so predators cannot easily see it.

Peregrine falcons do not build nests at all. They lay their eggs on high rocky ledges. Most other animals cannot reach these ledges, so the falcon eggs and chicks are safe there.

Golden eagles

Golden eagles are large, powerful birds of prey that are found in mountains in many parts of the world. They have big, sharp claws, called talons, which they use for catching their prey. They eat hares, marmots and other small mammals, and sometimes catch larger animals, such as young chamois. Golden eagles live in pairs and usually build their nests, called eyries, high up on rocky ledges.

The male eagle goes hunting and brings back food for the chicks.

The female eagle tears up meat for the chicks until they have learned how to feed themselves.

Golden eagle chicks

An eyrie is made of sticks and branches, and lined with dry mosses and grass.

Growing up

Golden eagles usually have two eggs at a time. The female guards the eggs, which take about six weeks to hatch.

One of the young chicks is bigger than the other. The two chicks fight each other, and the smaller one usually dies.

The chick that survives starts to grow brown feathers, called flight feathers, when it is four or five weeks old.

A few months later, the young eagle is big and strong enough to fly away. It leaves the nest to live on its own.

High fliers

Bar-headed geese breed in central Asia in the summer, and migrate over the Himalayas every year to spend the winter in northern India. They have been known to fly as high as 10,000m (33,000ft) - higher than Mount Everest.

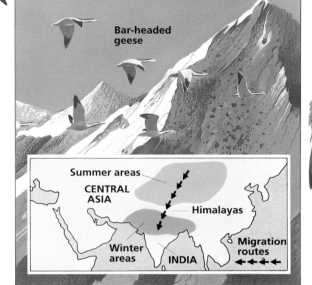

Bar-headed geese

Summer areas
CENTRAL ASIA
Himalayas
Winter areas
INDIA
Migration routes

Scavengers

Sometimes, meat-eaters feed on animals that have already died, instead of killing them themselves. This is called scavenging. Lots of mountain birds are scavengers. They eat animals that have fallen on the rocks.

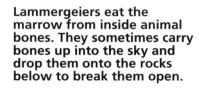

Lammergeier

Lammergeiers eat the marrow from inside animal bones. They sometimes carry bones up into the sky and drop them onto the rocks below to break them open.

Griffon vulture scavenging

Griffon vultures eat as much as they can, in case they do not find any more food for a while. They often eat so much that they are too full to fly away immediately.

Amazing birds of the Andes

The Andes mountains in South America are home to some of the world's largest and smallest birds. Huge Andean condors fly among the mountain peaks, and tiny hummingbirds live in the meadows and forests lower down.

Andean condor

Sparkling violetear hummingbird

Sparkling violetear hummingbirds are about 13cm (5in) long. They use their long beaks to suck a sweet liquid, called nectar, out of flowers.

Andean condors are the biggest birds of prey in the world. They can weigh up to 12.5kg (27lb) and measure over 120cm (47in) from the tips of their beaks to the ends of their tails.

Andean condor

Sparkling violetear hummingbird

Andean condors are almost a thousand times heavier than sparkling violetear hummingbirds.

The mountains of China

In the mountainous Sichuan area of central China, the weather is always damp and misty. Thick forests of trees and bamboo plants grow on the steep slopes. These forests are home to many rare animal species, such as pandas and golden monkeys.

CHINA Sichuan

Giant pandas

Giant pandas are rare relatives of bears. There are only about 700 of them left in the wild. They live mainly in Sichuan in the cool, damp forests, feeding on bamboo stems and leaves. They also eat other kinds of plants, small mammals, birds, fish and eggs. Giant pandas do not hibernate, but when it is very cold, they shelter in caves or hollow trees.

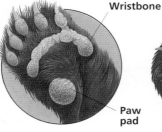
Wristbone

Paw pad

Giant pandas have five fingers on each front paw. They also have an extra large wristbone, which they use like a thumb to grip bamboo while they are eating it.

Giant pandas

Giant pandas mate in spring. When a female is ready to mate, she bleats and leaves her scent on trees to attract a male.

When a male panda is attracted, he answers her with high-pitched calls. The two pandas play together before they mate.

About five months later, the female makes a den in a cave, where she gives birth to one or two tiny, blind cubs.

The mother only cares for one of the cubs, so the other one dies. The cub that survives starts to grow fur after about ten days.

Young giant pandas are very playful. They often roll on their backs while they feed. They stay with their mothers for about 18 months.

Bamboo

When bamboo plants flower, the stems and leaves die, so giant pandas cannot always find enough to eat. For example, in Sichuan in 1983, a large area of bamboo flowered and died. Many giant pandas died as a result.

Sichuan species

Here are some of the other animals that live in the mountains of Sichuan.

Golden monkeys live in forests where there are lots of oak and chestnut trees. The fur on their backs can be up to 10cm (4in) long.

Golden monkey

Takin

Takins have long, shaggy coats. They live in bamboo forests and give out a strong, oily smell from all over their bodies.

Red pandas are distant relatives of giant pandas. They usually come out at night to eat fruit, roots, bamboo and other plants. Scientists think they may eat meat too.

Red panda

Musk deer

Giant pandas have two different kinds of teeth. They use their sharp front teeth for biting, and their hard, flat back teeth for chewing bamboo.

Small, shy musk deer live in forests. They eat grass, leaves, mosses and lichens. The males have long, sharp front teeth, which they use for fighting other males.

Pheasants

There are about 50 species of pheasants in the world. Many of these come from Sichuan. The pheasants shown here live in forests near the treeline. Males usually have brighter feathers than females.

Brown eared pheasant

Lady Amherst's pheasant

Common pheasant

Blood pheasant

Reeve's pheasant

Chinese Monal pheasant

Golden pheasant

Spring in the Alps

The Alps are a big range of mountains in Europe. During winter, they are almost completely covered in snow. When spring begins, some of the snow melts. As sunshine warms the damp ground, small plants start growing. Animals that have been asleep all winter come out of their burrows to find food. Other animals, such as chamois, come up from the forests to the meadows and rocky slopes that were covered in snow in winter. Many animals give birth in spring. It is easier for their babies to find food and keep warm at this time of year.

In warmer weather, the snow lower down the mountain melts. This means that the snowline is higher up in spring than it is in winter.

Snowline in spring

Snowline in winter

Young golden eagle

Golden eagles and other birds of prey fly high in the sky, looking for small mammals on the ground.

Alpine choughs can live very high up in the Alps. They eat insects and seeds.

Alpine chough

Female chamois and their babies, called kids, live together in herds. Kids stay with their mothers for about two years.

Herd of chamois

Female chamois

Chamois kid

In spring, mountain hares have a mixture of brown and white fur. Their white winter coats are gradually turning brown for the summer, so that the hares will be camouflaged among rocks and plants.

Mountain hare

Insects, such as butterflies and bees, fly close to the ground, feeding on nectar from flowers.

Honeybee

Alpine salamanders eat insects and slugs. They hide under stones, only coming out after showers of rain.

Spotted fritillary butterfly

Small Apollo butterfly

Alpine salamander

Swallowtail butterfly

Spotted fritillaries

Spotted fritillary butterflies pair up and mate in spring. Then the female lays her eggs on a small plant.

After a few days, caterpillars hatch out of the eggs. During the summer, they feed on the leaves of the plant.

In the autumn, each caterpillar grows a hard outer covering, called a pupa. This protects it during the harsh winter.

Inside the pupa, the caterpillar slowly changes into a butterfly. In spring, the butterfly comes out and looks for a mate.

Alpine marmots

Marmots come out of their burrows to look for plants to eat.

Gentian

Yellow mountain saxifrage

Spring flowers

Many mountain plants flower in spring. They grow mainly in the meadows and among the rocks. Some plants are very rare, so there are laws to stop people from picking them. They are called protected plants. These pictures show some of the flowers that grow in the Alps in spring.

Gentian

Edelweiss

Rock soapwort

Bear's-ear

Alpine aster

Yellow mountain saxifrage

Purple saxifrage

Mountain buttercup

Mountain avens

Alpine soldanellas can grow above the snowline. They give out heat as they grow. This melts the snow so the flowers can come through.

Alpine soldanellas

27

People in the mountains

Most mountain people live in tiny villages, far away from cities and towns. Many of them are farmers. They keep herds of animals and grow crops on the steep slopes. Life in a high mountain village can be very hard. The weather is often extremely cold, and above the treeline there are no trees for firewood. It is difficult to grow crops because the soil is thin and stony and is easily washed down the mountainside by the rain.

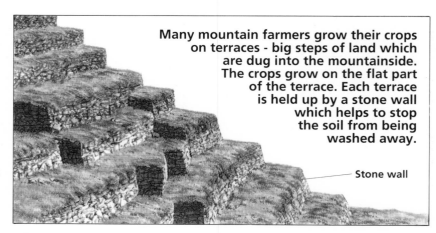

Many mountain farmers grow their crops on terraces - big steps of land which are dug into the mountainside. The crops grow on the flat part of the terrace. Each terrace is held up by a stone wall which helps to stop the soil from being washed away.

Stone wall

Sherpas

The Sherpas live in villages in the Himalayas, the highest mountains in the world. Most Sherpas live in Nepal. They grow rice and potatoes on their farms, and keep yaks as farm animals. They make butter and cheese out of yak milk, and use yak skin and wool to make clothes. Yak dung (droppings) is used instead of firewood.

Temple

There is a temple in every village. Most people pray there every day.

Sherpa houses are usually made of stone, with very thick walls to keep out the cold. The animals live in stables downstairs, and the people live upstairs. The warmth from the animals' bodies helps to heat the house.

Rooms upstairs for people

Stables downstairs for animals

Yak

During the day, the yaks wander around, feeding on grass. They are put back into their stables at night.

Sherpa children often have to help their parents by doing farm work, but today, most of them go to school as well. They sometimes have their lessons outside.

Many Sherpas work as guides, or porters, for tourists and climbers. They show people the safest paths to use in the mountains, and help them carry their heavy bags.

Mountain climbing

People climb mountains as a sport, or to see the wildlife there. A climb to the top of a mountain is called an ascent. In 1953, Edmund Hillary, a climber from New Zealand, and Tenzing Norgay, a Sherpa porter, made the first ascent of Everest. They were with a group of climbers, but only Hillary and Tenzing got to the top.

This picture shows the route Hillary and Tenzing took.

FINISH

Mount Everest

⟋ Hillary and Tenzing's route

▲ Camp

For their ascent, Hillary and Tenzing wore special boots to stop them from slipping. They took ice axes, for climbing on ice, and oxygen, to help them breathe.

The ascent took several weeks, so the climbers had to stop at camps on the way.

START

Base camp

The base camp was the starting point for the ascent.

Abominable snowmen

Many people believe that a strange kind of animal, called the Yeti, lives in the Himalayas. It is sometimes called the abominable snowman. Lots of big footprints have been found, but nobody has ever caught a Yeti or found a dead one. In North America, people believe in a similar creature, which they call Bigfoot.

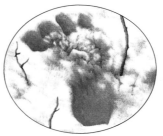

Lots of people have seen footprints like this one. They are usually about 32cm (13in) long - bigger than most people's feet.

This is what some people think the Yeti, or Bigfoot, might look like. It is much bigger than a human, and covered in shaggy hair.

Peaceful places

People who want a peaceful life often go to live in the mountains. Monks are men who spend their lives praying and learning about their religion. They live in buildings called monasteries, which are often built on mountains. There, the monks can live in peace and quiet, far away from noisy towns.

Monastery

The picture on the right shows a monastery in the Pindus mountains in Greece. It is built on a high pillar of rock.

Mountains in danger

Mountains are usually far away from the busy areas where most people live, but mountain plants and animals are still in danger from some of the things that people do, such as chopping down trees and hunting. Even in areas where there are very few people, pollution carried in the air can destroy habitats and kill wildlife. Today, many people are trying to protect mountain areas and the wildlife living there from these dangers.

Endangered species

Plants and animals that are in danger of dying out are called endangered species. Many mountain species are endangered because the forests where they live are chopped down to make room for farms or houses. Some mountain animals are hunted by people for their skins, or for other parts of their bodies. People also pick plants and flowers for collections, or to make medicines.

Snow leopards are endangered because people hunt them for their fur, although this is against the law. Some snow leopards are kept in zoos, where they can live safely and breed. This helps them to increase their numbers. It is called captive breeding.

Snow leopard

Radio tracking

Scientists need to learn about wildlife before they can protect it. One way of finding out how animals live is by following, or tracking, their movements. These pictures show how a scientist tracks a snow leopard.

The scientist drugs the snow leopard to make it go to sleep for a short time. While it is asleep, a radio collar is fastened around its neck.

When the snow leopard wakes up and starts to move around, the transmitter on the collar sends out invisible radio signals through the air.

The scientist uses a receiver to pick up these signals. The receiver makes beeping noises. By listening to these, the scientist can tell where the snow leopard is.

Trees in trouble

People cut down trees for wood, or so they can use the land for farming. Cutting down large areas of forest is called deforestation. On mountains, this can be especially dangerous. The trees' roots hold soil in place on the mountainside. If the trees are cut down, rain can wash the soil down the mountain causing landslides. It may also block rivers and cause floods.

This picture shows a mountainside in Nepal. Many trees have been cut down, so there is nothing to stop the rain from washing away the soil. Once the soil has gone, the land is no good for growing crops.

In the 1970s, women in Nepal and India hugged trees to stop other people from cutting them down. This was called the Chipko movement. Soon, people in other countries began to do the same thing.

Pollution on the move

Forests, rivers and lakes can be damaged by acid rain and snow. These are caused by pollution, which may come from cities many miles away.

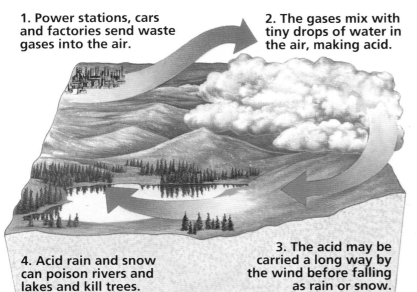

1. Power stations, cars and factories send waste gases into the air.

2. The gases mix with tiny drops of water in the air, making acid.

3. The acid may be carried a long way by the wind before falling as rain or snow.

4. Acid rain and snow can poison rivers and lakes and kill trees.

Protecting wildlife

Many groups of people are working to protect mountain areas and the plants and animals living there. They try to save endangered species, and to stop hunting, pollution and deforestation. In some places, areas have been set aside where it is against the law to hunt animals or chop down trees. These protected areas are called wildlife parks or reserves.

These American children are protesting against the destruction of redwood forests. Redwoods are a kind of conifer tree.

Joining a group is one way of helping to protect animals and plants. Some groups have special wildlife clubs for children. People from anywhere in the world can join. Here are some addresses you can write to:

Young Ornithologists' Club, RSPB, The Lodge, Sandy, Bedfordshire SG19 2DL, UK

Go Wild! Club, WWF, Panda House, Weyside Park, Godalming, Surrey GU7 1XR, UK

World Wildlife Fund, 90 Eglington Ave. East, Toronto, Ontario M4P 2Z7, Canada

Lifewatch, London Zoo, Regents Park, London NW1 4RY, UK

Index

Photograph of Sherpa schoolchildren on page 28, © Joan Klatchko/Hutchison Library
Photograph of Sherpa porters on page 28, © Timothy Beddow/Hutchison Library
Photograph of Chipko woman on page 31, © R. Berridale-Johnson/Panos Pictures
Photograph of children demonstrating on page 31, © Daniel Dancer/STILL PICTURES
Use of RSPB logo on page 31, © RSPB. Use of WWF logo on page 31, © WWF.